The Little Match Girl

QUICK STARTER   250 HEADWORDS

OXFORD
UNIVERSITY PRESS

Great Clarendon Street, Oxford, OX2 6DP, United Kingdom

Oxford University Press is a department of the University of Oxford.
It furthers the University's objective of excellence in research, scholarship,
and education by publishing worldwide. Oxford is a registered trade
mark of Oxford University Press in the UK and in certain other countries

This edition © Oxford University Press 2012

The moral rights of the author have been asserted

First published in Dominoes 2012

2025 2024 2023 2022

14

ISBN: 978 0 19 424940 9   Book
ISBN: 978 0 19 463907 1   Book and Audio Pack
Audio not available separately

Printed in China

This book is printed on paper from certified and well-managed sources

ACKNOWLEDGEMENTS

Text adaptation by: Bill Bowler

Illustrations and cover by: Mónica Armiño

The publisher would also like to thank the following for permission to reproduce photographs:
Alamy p. 25 (Dana Hull/Everett Collection); Getty Images p. 24 (Hulton Archive).

DOMINOES

Series Editors: Bill Bowler and Sue Parminter

The Little Match Girl

Hans Christian Andersen

Text adaptation by Bill Bowler

Illustrated by Mónica Armiño

Hans Christian Andersen was born in the town of Odense, Denmark, in 1805. He was an only child, and came from a poor family. But he didn't want to stay and do ordinary work in Odense. He loved singing, storytelling, and the theatre. So at 14, he went to look for more interesting work in Copenhagen. There, the Danish King helped to pay for his education, and he became a writer. Hans Christian Andersen wrote poems, novels, and travel books, but he is most famous today for his many wonderful children's stories. He died in 1875, at a friend's house near Copenhagen, after a bad fall.

OXFORD
UNIVERSITY PRESS

Story Characters

The Little Match Girl

The Father

The Mother

The Grandmother

Contents

BEFORE READING

This story is about a poor little girl. What do you think happens in it? Tick the boxes.

a The girl … one cold December night.
  1 ☐ stays at home
  2 ☐ goes out

b She loses her … in the street.
  1 ☐ mother's shoes
  2 ☐ father's watch

c She … that evening.
  1 ☐ sells lots of matches
  2 ☐ doesn't sell any matches

d She eats … that night.
  1 ☐ a lot
  2 ☐ nothing

e She sees … things in her head.
  1 ☐ wonderful
  2 ☐ not very nice

f In the end, the girl … .
  1 ☐ dies
  2 ☐ lives in her grandmother's house

Chapter 1

Her cold little home

The little girl lives with her mother and father. The **wind** comes in through the **walls** of their cold little house.

'Anne Marie,' the girl's mother cries one day. 'We've got no money. Go out and **sell** some **matches**!'

'Yes, Mother,' her daughter says. She puts some matches into her old **apron**.

wind air that moves

wall the side of a house

sell to take money for something

match you light a fire, or a candle with this

apron you wear this over a dress to put things in

Then she puts her feet into some shoes near the front door.

'Don't come back without any money,' her father says. 'Or I'm taking my **belt** to your back!'
'No, Father,' the little girl answers. She remembers her father's last **beating**, and she is afraid.

belt you wear this round your middle

beating when you hit someone strongly

ACTIVITIES

READING CHECK

Correct the mistakes in the sentences.

father

a The little girl lives with her mother and ~~flower~~.

b They live in a cold little hotel.

c The girl wants to sell some watches.

d She puts them into her old apple.

e She puts her feet in some old shoes by the dog.

f She is afraid of her brother.

g He often takes his belt to her bag.

h The girl doesn't like his buildings.

i She must go back home with some matches.

GUESS WHAT

What does the little girl do in the next chapter? Tick one box.

a She sells lots of matches. ☐

b She sells no matches. ☐

c She finds some money. ☐

d She finds a little dog. ☐

3

Chapter 2

Her mother's shoes

The little girl opens the door. She goes out into the cold street. It is **snowing**.

The shoes on her feet are very big for her. That is because they are her mother's shoes.

When the little girl walks across the road, two **coaches** go past very quickly. 'Hey! Move!' cries one of the coach drivers angrily.

snow to rain something cold, and white; something soft, cold, and white

coach a kind of car with horses

She runs across the road.
The shoes **fall** from her feet.

She looks for them at
once. But she can't find
one shoe in the snow . . .

. . . and a street boy takes the second
shoe in his hands. 'When I'm older,
my children can sleep in this little
bed!' he laughs. Then he runs away
with the shoe.

fall to go down suddenly

The little girl now walks over the snow in her **bare** feet. They are very cold and blue.

'**Buy** my matches!' she cries. But nobody buys any matches from her. No one gives her any money.

It is very cold now. Snow is falling, and the sky is darker. It is the last night of the year.

bare with nothing on

buy to give money for something

ACTIVITIES

READING CHECK

Choose the correct words to complete these sentences.

a It is *raining* / *snowing* out in the street.

b The shoes on the little girl's feet are very *big* / *little* for her.

c They are her *mother's* / *sister's* shoes.

d When the girl is in the road, two *bicycles* / *coaches* go past.

e *'Hello! / Move!'* cries one of the coach drivers.

f The girl *runs* / *walks* across the road.

g She loses her *shoes* / *sandwiches* in the street.

h She sells *no* / *all her* matches that evening.

GUESS WHAT

What happens in the next chapter? Tick the boxes.

		Yes	No
a	The girl walks slowly through the streets.	☐	☐
b	She finds some money in the snow.	☐	☐
c	She sits down near two houses out of the wind.	☐	☐
d	She goes into a shop and buys some bread.	☐	☐
e	She gives the bread to hungry street children.	☐	☐
f	She is very cold and very hungry.	☐	☐
g	She goes home to her mother and father.	☐	☐
h	She stays out in the cold street.	☐	☐

Chapter 3

A corner to sit in

The **poor** little match girl is cold and hungry. So she walks slowly through the streets. What a **sad** picture! What a poor thing, with her bare head and bare feet! The snow falls on her beautiful, long, yellow hair.

poor without money; something you say when you feel sorry for someone

sad not happy

There are **lights** in all the windows. There is a wonderful **smell** of **roast goose**, too. This is because it is the night of 31st December – New Year's Eve.

Just then, the girl sees a little house near a bigger house in front of her. The walls of the two houses make a **corner** in the street.

light a thing that helps you to see in the dark; to give fire to something

smell something that your nose tells you; to tell your nose something

roast cooked in the oven

goose (*plural* **geese**) a large, usually white bird; people eat it at Christmas or New Year in different countries

corner where two walls meet

She goes and sits there out of the wind. She puts her little feet under her. She is colder now.

'But I can't go home with no money,' she thinks. 'I don't want a beating.'

The little girl's hands are very cold and white now. 'What can I do?' she thinks.

'I know. I can take one little match and **strike** it **against** the wall. Perhaps then my cold hands can be warmer.'

strike to hit on something (of a match) to make it burn

against on, or just next to

ACTIVITIES

READING CHECK

Correct nine more mistakes in the story.

hungry

The poor little match girl is cold and ~~thirsty~~. She walks slowly through the
shops. Her head and feet are bare. The snow falls on her beautiful long red
hair. It's a very sad picture. There are lights in all the doors. And, because
it's New Year's Eve, there's a wonderful smell of roast dog, too.

Just then, the girl sees a big and a little hotel in front of her. Their walls
meet and make a corner out of the sun. At once, the little girl goes and
sits in this corner. She puts her little hands under her. There, in the corner,
she feels colder. What can she do? She has no milk and so she doesn't want
to go home. She doesn't want a bottle from her father. Perhaps she can
strike a match and be warm again?

GUESS WHAT

What happens in the next chapter? Tick three sentences.

a ☐ The girl strikes a match.
b ☐ Her father comes and looks for her.
c ☐ He gives a beating to his daughter.
d ☐ She is warmer for a time.
e ☐ She sees a roast goose in someone's house.
f ☐ She goes through the window and eats it.

The little girl takes a match. She strikes it against the wall. R-r-ritch! It makes a nice noise, and gives a good light, too. The **flame** is yellow and warm. The little girl puts her cold hand over it.

flame the light that you see when something is on fire

In its light, she sees a hot **stove** in front of her. It is big, new – and beautiful!

She puts her cold feet near the nice warm stove . . .

. . . but then the little flame dies. The stove goes from before her eyes. Now she's got only a **burnt** match in her hand.

stove a big metal box with fire in that makes a room warm

burnt made black by fire

Again she takes a match. She strikes it against the wall of the house. The light from it falls on the wall. Suddenly the girl can see into the room behind.

On the table there is a snow-white **cloth**, and on this there are beautiful **plates**. A roast goose is sitting on the biggest plate. It smells wonderful.

Just then, the goose **jumps** down and walks across to the little girl. It has a big **knife** and **fork** in its back.

cloth you put this on a table for an important dinner

plate you put things to eat on this

jump to move fast on your legs from one thing to a different thing

knife you cut things to eat with this

fork you hold things to eat when you cut them, and put them in your mouth with this

14

READING CHECK

Put these sentences in the correct order. Number them 1–10.

a ☐ A roast goose jumps off the table and walks to the girl.
b ☐ In the light of the match, she sees a stove in front of her.
c ☐ She puts her cold feet near the stove.
d ☐ She puts her cold hand over the warm flame.
e ☐ The flame of the first match dies.
f ☐ The girl sees into the room behind the wall.
g ☐ The girl strikes a second match against the wall.
h ☐ The girl strikes the first match against the wall.
i ☐ The light from the second match falls on the wall.
j ☐ The stove goes from before the girl's eyes.

GUESS WHAT

What happens in the next chapter? Tick one box to finish each sentence.

a The goose …
   1 ☐ goes when the flame of the second match dies.
   2 ☐ runs away down the street.
   3 ☐ talks to the girl.

b The girl …
   1 ☐ remembers her grandfather.
   2 ☐ runs down the street after the goose.
   3 ☐ strikes another match against the wall.

c The match …
   1 ☐ kills the girl in its flames.
   2 ☐ brings more wonderful things before the girl's eyes.
   3 ☐ falls in the snow.

But then the flame from the second match dies. Now the little girl can see only the cold house wall in front of her.

She lights a third match. Now she is sitting under the most beautiful **Christmas** tree. It is bigger and nicer than the one in the window of the old **merchant**'s home last Christmas.

There are thousands of **candles** all over the green tree. And there are beautiful little pictures in different colours, too. The little girl puts out her hand for them.

Christmas 25th December, a holiday to remember when Jesus was born

merchant a person who buys and sells things

candle it burns and gives light; in the past people used them to see at night

16

Then the flame of the match dies. But the Christmas lights stay. They go up before the girl's eyes. She sees them now up in the sky: they are the **stars**.

Just then, a star falls. It makes a yellow **line** across the sky.

star a far away sun that we see as a little light in the night sky

line a long, thin mark

'Someone is dying,' the little girl thinks. She remembers her grandmother, and the old woman's love for her.

The **kind** old woman is now dead. But the little girl can't forget her grandmother's **words** to her, 'When a star falls, a **soul** is going up to **God**.'

kind nice to people

word a thing that you say or write

soul the part of the person that is not the body; some people think it leaves the body when a person dies

God an important being who never dies, and who decides what happens in the world

READING CHECK

Choose the correct pictures.

a What does the little girl see in the light of the third match?

  1 ☑ a Christmas tree

  2 ☐ Father Christmas

b What does she see on the tree?

  1 ☐ snow

  2 ☐ candles

c What does she put out her hand for?

  1 ☐ black-and-white photos

  2 ☐ colour pictures

d What does the girl see when the third match dies?

  1 ☐ the stars in the sky

  2 ☐ the wall

e Who does the girl remember when a star falls?

  1 ☐ her grandmother

  2 ☐ her grandfather

GUESS WHAT

What happens in the next chapter? Circle the words to complete the sentences.

a The little girl sees her *grandfather* / *grandmother*.

b She strikes *all the* / *no more* matches on the wall.

c She doesn't want to *lose* / *see* her grandmother again.

d The old woman takes the girl *home* / *up into the sky*.

e The girl is very *happy* / *afraid* in the end.

Again the little girl strikes a match on the wall.

In its light, she suddenly sees her grandmother.
'Oh, Grandmother! It's you!' the child cries.
'Please don't go away when the match flame dies.'

She quickly lights lots of matches. She doesn't want to lose her grandmother again. And all the matches make a big, yellow flame – lighter than the day.

Now the old woman is taller and more beautiful than before. 'Grandmother, please take me with you!' the girl cries.

Then the grandmother takes the little girl in her arms. They **fly** up happily into the sky. They aren't cold, or hungry, or afraid now – because they are with God.

fly to move through the air

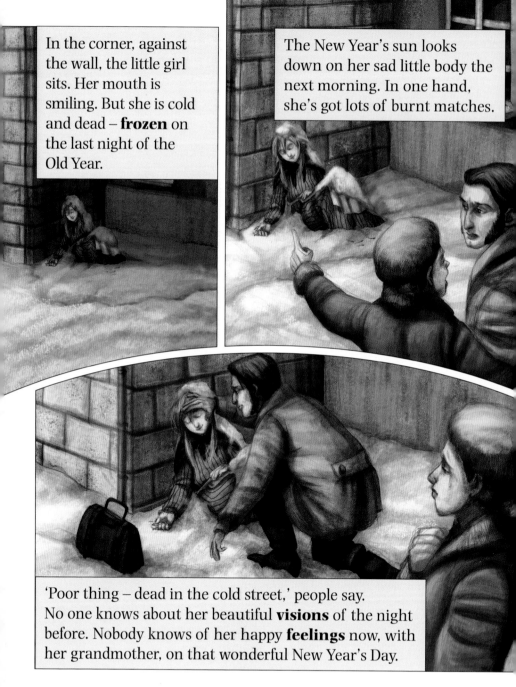

In the corner, against the wall, the little girl sits. Her mouth is smiling. But she is cold and dead – **frozen** on the last night of the Old Year.

The New Year's sun looks down on her sad little body the next morning. In one hand, she's got lots of burnt matches.

'Poor thing – dead in the cold street,' people say. No one knows about her beautiful **visions** of the night before. Nobody knows of her happy **feelings** now, with her grandmother, on that wonderful New Year's Day.

frozen not moving because very cold (under 0°C)

vision something that you see in your head

feeling something that you feel in you

READING CHECK

Are these sentences true or false? Tick the boxes.

		True	False
a	The little girl strikes a match against the ground.	☐	☑
b	She sees her grandmother in the light of the match.	☐	☐
c	The girl doesn't want to lose the old woman again.	☐	☐
d	The little girl lights lots of candles.	☐	☐
e	The grandmother is taller and more beautiful than before.	☐	☐
f	The grandmother takes the girl in her arms.	☐	☐
g	They fly up sadly into the sky.	☐	☐
h	The next day, people find the dead grandmother in the street.	☐	☐
i	They are happy for her.	☐	☐

GUESS WHAT

What does the girl's soul do after the story finishes? Tick the boxes and add your own ideas.

a ☐ It stays with her grandmother up in the sky.
b ☐ It plays all day and never works again.
c ☐ It talks to God.
d ☐ It visits her old home.
e ☐ It tells her father, 'Never hit a child again!'
f ☐ It tells her mother, 'Money isn't everything.'
g ☐ It helps different street children.
h ☐ ....
i ☐ ....

23

Project A   *Famous children's stories*

1   Read the text about *The Little Match Girl* and complete the table with notes.

The Little Match Girl (1845) is a story by Hans Christian Andersen, a Danish writer (1805–1875). People know him all over the world today for his wonderful fairy tales. Odense in Denmark is Andersen's home town. There are different films of the story. These include a short film made by Walt Disney in 2006. These days you can visit a *Little Match Girl* attraction in the Fairy Tale Forest. This is part of the Efteling theme park, in the Netherlands.

Story and date	
Author's name, nationality, and dates	
Famous for	
Home town	
Film versions of the story	
Things to do connected with the story	

PROJECTS

2 Read the notes about the story *The Wonderful Wizard of Oz,* and complete the text about the story.

Story and date	The Wonderful Wizard of Oz, 1900
Author's name, nationality, and dates	Lyman Frank Baum, American, 1856–1919
Famous for	Stories about Oz
Home town	Village of Chittenango in New York State, USA
Film versions of the story	A movie – The Wizard of Oz – starring Judy Garland, 1939
Things to do connected with the story	'Oz-Stravaganza', a three-day festival every June, in Chittenango to celebrate Baum's writing

The .... is a story

by ...., an .... writer.

He was born in .... and he died in ....

People know him all over the world today for his .... about

.... The village of ...., in ....

.... State, is Baum's .... town.

There are different films of the story including a movie

made in .... which stars ....

....

These days you can go to the ....

.... – a .... -day ....

every ...., in the village of ....

It celebrates .... 's writing.

3 Find out more about one of these stories and write a short text about it.

Peter Pan   The Little Prince   The Snow Queen

The Adventures of Pinocchio   Heidi

25

Project B *Writing a monologue*

> **A monologue** is a play, or part of a play, when only one character speaks.

1 Read this monologue. Which part of *The Little Match Girl* story is it about?

> **ANDERS:** It's late afternoon. I'm at home. I'm not working these days. I can hear and feel the cold December wind. It's coming through the thin walls of our little house. I'm sitting at the table with my wife, Anna. I can smell her dirty old dress and long, dirty hair. I'm tired and angry. I can see our daughter, Anne Marie. She's standing at the front door. She's opening it, and she's going out into the street. I'm thinking about finding work and making some money.

Part of story (chapter, page, and picture):

. . . .

2 Write notes about the monologue in the table.

Who is the speaker?	
Where is he?	
What is he doing?	
What is happening around him?	
What can he hear, see, smell and feel?	
What are his feelings?	
What is he thinking about?	

3 Think of a different part of the story of *The Little Match Girl*. Write notes for a
   monologue about it in the table below.

Who are you?	
Where are you?	
What are you doing?	
What is happening around you?	
What can you hear, see, smell, and feel?	
What are your feelings?	
What are you thinking about?	

4 Write a monologue using your notes from Activity 3. Read it aloud.
   Your classmates must guess which part of the story it comes from.

WORD WORK 1

1 Find words in the shoes to match the pictures.

a chaco   **b** telb   **c** panor

........coach.......   ....

 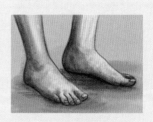

d tcham   **e** lawl   **f** reba

....

2 Complete the sentences with words from Chapters 1 and 2.

a Can you hear the noise of the .....wind..... tonight?

b Why do apples .... from trees?

c The street's all white. It has .... on it.

d How much is this book? I'd like to .... it.

e My dad wants to .... his car. He needs the money.

f I give her a .... when she does something wrong.

28

WORD WORK 2

1 Look at the pictures. Complete the crossword with words from Chapters 3 and 4.

ACROSS

1

2

4

7

DOWN

1

3

5

6

1 p l a t e

2 Complete each sentence with a word from the box.

| against | burnt | corner | jumping | light | ~~roast~~ | smell | strike |

a This .....roast..... goose is wonderful!

b That bread is .... Look! It's all black.

c I can't see a thing in the dark. I need a ....

d Ugh! There's a .... of smoke in the house!

e She's sitting over there in the .... of the room.

f Children, stop .... up and down on your beds!

g Let's put our bicycles .... the wall.

h Can you .... a match?

WORD WORK 3

1 These words don't match the pictures. Correct them.

a   Christmas

......frozen......

b   candle

....

c   frozen

....

d   line

....

e   fly

....

f   star

....

2 Complete the sentences with words from Chapters 5 and 6.

a He buys and sells things in Venice. He's a m e r c h a n t .

b Is this Danish? I can't understand a _ _ _ _ of it.

c My grandfather helps me a lot. He's very _ _ _ _ to me.

d When things are very bad, we sometimes ask _ _ _ for help.

e Let's buy this house! I have a good _ _ _ _ _ _ _ _ about it.

f Sometimes I see _ _ _ _ _ _ _ _ of things before they happen.

g Some people say that when you die, your _ _ _ _ leaves your body.

GRAMMAR

GRAMMAR CHECK

Adjectives and adverbs of manner

We use adjectives to describe things or people. They tell us more about <u>nouns</u>.

It's a cold <u>night</u>.   *The <u>sky</u> is dark.*

We use adverbs of manner to talk about how we do things. They tell us more about <u>verbs</u>.

The girl's mother <u>talks</u> to her coldly.

Her father <u>looks</u> at her darkly.

To make regular adverbs, we add –ly to the adjective.

cold – coldly

Adjectives that end in –y, we change to –ily.

angry – angrily

Some adverbs are irregular.

He runs fast. (adjective fast)   *He speaks French well. (adjective good)*

1 Circle the correct word to complete each sentence.

a The girl answers her mother and father *nice /* (*nicely*)

b She's a *quietly / quiet* girl.

c Two coaches go past very *fast / fastly*.

d She looks *careful / carefully* for her shoes in the snow.

e She walks *slow / slowly* through the streets on bare feet.

f The merchant has a *beautiful / beautifully* Christmas tree.

g The girl looks at the roast goose *hungrily / hungryly*.

h *Sudden / Suddenly* the girl sees her grandmother.

i She remembers the old woman *good / well*.

j The girl is *happy / happily* when her soul is with God.

k People are *sad / sadly* when they see her dead body.

l She has a *wonderful / wonderfully* time with her grandmother.

GRAMMAR CHECK

To + infinitive or *–ing* form of verb

After the verbs *forget*, *learn*, *need*, *remember*, *want,* and *would like*, we use *to* + infinitive.

She'd like to have a Christmas tree.

After the verbs *finish*, *go*, *like*, *love*, and *stop*, we use verb + *–ing*.

She loves looking into the flames.

With the verbs *begin* and *like*, we can use to + infinitive or verb + *–ing*.

2 **Complete these sentences about the story with the *to* + infinitive or *–ing* form of the verbs in brackets.**

a Anne Marie would like . . . . to play . . . (play) all day.

b She learns . . . . (sell) matches from her mother.

c She begins . . . . (make) money when she's very little.

d Her father likes . . . . (hit) her.

e She leaves when her father finishes . . . . (talk) to her.

f She needs . . . . (wear) her mother's shoes.

g She remembers . . . . (put) some matches in her apron.

h She doesn't forget . . . . (close) the door behind her.

i She loves . . . . (look) in shop windows.

j She doesn't want . . . . (go) home with no money.

k She stops . . . . (walk) when she sees a corner out of the wind.

l She doesn't like . . . . (be) cold and hungry.

m She doesn't want . . . . (lose) her grandmother.

n In the end, she goes . . . . (fly) up into the sky.

GRAMMAR CHECK

Present Simple: Negative

We make most Present Simple verbs negative with *doesn't* (*does not*) or *don't* (*do not*) + infinitive without to.

The little girl doesn't (does not) live in a big house.

With the verbs *be*, *have got* and *can*, we add n't (not) to the verb.

They aren't (are not) very nice to her.

Her mother and father haven't (have not) got lots of money.

3 Write a negative and an affirmative sentence each time. Change the <u>underlined</u> words.

a Anne Marie has got a <u>new</u> apron.

Anne Marie hasn't got a new apron. She's got an old apron.

b She's wearing her mother's <u>coat</u>.

....

c Two <u>cars</u> go past.

....

d The <u>matches</u> fall in the road.

....

e She's got <u>black</u> hair.

....

f It's <u>Christmas</u> Eve.

....

g The <u>doors</u> have got lights in.

....

h She <u>stands</u> in a corner.

....

i There are candles on the <u>table</u>.

....

j A <u>plane</u> falls from the sky.

....

k There are burnt <u>pictures</u> in her hand.

....

DOMINOES Your Choice

Read *Dominoes* for pleasure, or to develop language skills. It's your choice.

Each *Domino* reader includes:
- a good story to enjoy
- integrated activities to develop reading skills and increase vocabulary
- task-based projects – perfect for CEFR portfolios
- contextualized grammar activities

Each *Domino* pack contains a reader, and an excitingly dramatized audio recording of the story

If you liked this *Domino*, read these:

The Selfish Giant
Oscar Wilde

'It's my garden,' says the Giant. 'People must understand. Nobody can play here – only me!'

So the children leave, and the Selfish Giant puts a wall around his garden. After that, it's always winter there.

Later, the Giant feels sorry for a young boy in the snow. He knocks down the garden wall – and the children, and the spring, come back. But where is the young boy now? And how can the Giant find him again?

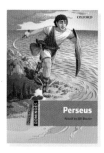

Perseus
Retold by Bill Bowler

Perseus is the son of Danae, Princess of Argos, and the god Zeus. When he is very young, his mother moves with him to live on the island of Seriphos.

Later, Polydectes – the king of Seriphos – wants to marry Danae. Perseus says 'no' to this, so Polydectes sends the young man away for the head of Medusa. Medusa is a she-monster, with snakes for hair. Can Perseus find and kill Medusa? And what happens after he goes back to Seriphos?

	CEFR	Cambridge Exams	IELTS	TOEFL iBT	TOEIC
Level 3	B1	PET	4.0	57-86	550
Level 2	A2–B1	KET-PET	3.0-4.0	–	390
Level 1	A1–A2	YLE Flyers/KET	3.0	–	225
Starter & Quick Starter	A1	YLE Movers	1.0–2.0	–	–

You can find details and a full list of books and teachers' resources on our website:
www.oup.com/elt/gradedreaders